THE
HUNGRY
DRAGON

WANDA PIERPOINT

Illustrated by Jo Allsopp and Sandra Leckie

ISBN 978-1-78996-032-7

APS Publications,

4 Oakleigh Road, Stourbridge, West Midlands, DY8 2JX

www.andrewsparke.com

Chapter One

The dragon sniffed the air. Food! The delicious smell of young children. Grown-ups were no good. They were stringy and tough but children were different. Their flesh was so tender and sweet and their bones crunchy and juicy. He started to dribble and the spit dropped onto the ground.

He looked around his field. There was little of interest to eat. The rabbits had all gone. Hedgehogs were alright but the spines hurt his throat. There were no birds nesting in the hedgerows. Really there were only worms and beetles and he was a DRAGON! It was beneath him to scrabble around in the dirt to look for the odd worm or insect. He sniffed the air again.

Nobody knew that the dragon was there. Nobody thought he could be there because dragons do not exist, except in fairy stories – but he was there, in a field next to the playing field of a primary school. At the back of the playing field was a hedge with a gate set in the middle. Through the gate was a lane with tall hedges on either side hiding the fields – and in the right hand field lived the dragon.

All day long the dragon could hear children, smell children and, if he peered through the hedge, he could see children.

However the dragon was clever. He knew that if he jumped over the hedge and caught a child he would be seen and then, no matter how fast he was, some child would escape and tell the grown-ups that a dragon was loose. Then he would be captured and maybe killed. So, although he was very hungry, he waited and waited until he could find a child on its own.

Chapter Two

Most of the children at the school went home by the front entrance. Their parents would be waiting at the school gate to collect them and take them home. Some children, however, used the lane at the back of the school to go home as they lived in the farms and cottages nearby – and the lane went past the field where the dragon lived.

Billy Brewster was one of the children who went home down the lane. He was the type of boy who was always in a mess. He would pick up the wrong exercise book; sit at the wrong table; forget his homework. He was going home with his friends when he suddenly remembered that his mum had told him to bring his dirty P.E. kit home. Normally this would not have worried him but she had also told him that if he forgot again he wouldn't be allowed to go on his x-box. So he went back into the cloakroom to fetch it. Naturally it was not hanging up on his peg and by the time he had found it – stuffed under the bench – all the other children had left.

As Billy walked down the lane the dragon sniffed the air. A child – a tender, juicy child. He listened carefully. There were no other footsteps. The child was alone. The dragon smiled his fearsome dragon smile, soared over the trees and landed in front of Billy. Billy opened his mouth in amazement. The dragon opened his mouth in anticipation and out shot flames which surrounded Billy and cooked him to perfection. He curled out his tongue, picked up Billy and swallowed him whole. Crunch, crunch, crunch. Delicious! He then spat out Billy's P.E. kit and dug a hole with his claw. He put the smelly P.E .kit in the hole and covered it up. Then he flew back over the trees to his field and for the first time in ages went to sleep with a full tummy.

Chapter Three

Sally Spencer had long blond hair which was always neatly tied up in bunches on the side of her head. She had large blue eyes and rosy cheeks. She wasn't very clever but she was so sweet and good that nobody seemed to notice. She would stand, looking bewildered, with her blue eyes growing bigger and bigger until the grown-ups would pat her on the head and tell her not to worry. So she didn't.

A few days after Billy disappeared Sally was going home down the lane with her friends when she noticed that there was a dirty mark on her shoe. She stopped to wipe it off with a tissue. (Sally was the type of child who always carried tissues!) Unfortunately it left a smudgy mark. She dipped the corner of her tissue into a puddle of rain water and cleaned it.

Then she dried it with a second tissue. When her shoe was totally clean she stood up. Her friends were out of sight but in front of her was a large dragon. Sally made her blue eyes go bigger. The dragon smiled. Sally made a little O shape with her mouth. The dragon opened his mouth and breathed out fire which surrounded Sally and cooked her to perfection. His long tongue encircled her and drew her to his mouth. Crunch,

crunch, crunch. Delicious. He didn't even have to spit out her P.E. bag. It tasted of rose petals. (Smelly washing powder). Once again the dragon slept well with a full tummy.

During the next few weeks the dragon managed to eat three more children who travelled down the lane on their own. Three times he went to sleep with a smile on his face and a contented tummy. He began to think of the field as his home and the school as his food cupboard.

Chapter Four

At first the mothers of the missing children were not too concerned when their children didn't come home. After all the bedrooms stayed tidy and the biscuit tins still had some biscuits in them at the end of the week. But after a while they began to wonder what had happened to their offspring and, being sensible parents,

they went to see the Headmaster, Mr Mealing.

Mr Mealing sat them down in his office and listened to their concerns. Then he looked at the registers and said,

 "Well your children were in school but when they did not come back we thought that they were ill or on holiday. Leave it with me and I will try and find out what happened to them when they left school."

The mums were very happy to do this as Mr Mealing was a very clever man so they left and went back to their very tidy and quiet houses.

Mr Mealing looked very carefully at the registers and after a while he realised that all the missing children went home down the lane at the back of the playing fields. There was no problem with the children who were collected by their parents at the front of the school. So something was happening to the Lane children.

Next morning, in Assembly, he announced to the whole school.

"Nobody, and I mean NOBODY, is to go down the lane on their own. They are to go with their friends or with an adult. If you are on your own you are to come back into school and get a teacher to walk down with you. Do you understand?"

The children droned back, "Yes Mr Mealing."

"If anyone disobeys they will be in serious trouble. Do you understand me?"

"Yes Mr Mealing."

When Mr Mealing was sure that no child would go down the lane on their own he went back to his office for the next part of his plan. He wrote down an advertisement to go into the local paper.

Wanted

A man who looks like a boy and who can do karate

Good rate of pay

Might be dangerous

The day after the advert had appeared in the paper there were two people waiting outside the headmaster's office waiting to be interviewed for the job.

They were both small and one had long brown hair, a moustache and a beard. The second had short fair hair. Mr Mealing asked the person with the beard to come into his office.

"Good morning," welcomed Mr Mealing. "What is your name and what can you do?"

"I am Mr Brown," said Mr Brown. "I am very fit and I can do karate."

"Can you show me?"

Mr Brown stood up and swept his right hand across the table knocking all Mr Mealing's books and papers onto the floor. Then he picked up a chair and threw it across the room where it smashed into the cabinet that contained the school sports' trophies. Glass flew everywhere and the cabinet started to rock forward.

Mr Mealing dashed forward and stopped it crashing to the ground. He then turned and looked very closely at Mr Brown.

"Do I know you?" he asked.

"No," replied Mr Brown. "I have never met you before."

"I am sure that I have seen you before."

"Never," stammered Mr Brown.

"I am positive that you are familiar. Something about the way you threw the chair."

Then Mr Mealing reached over, grabbed Mr Brown's hair and yanked.

"Ow!" yelled Mr Brown and reached up to stop the headmaster but it was too late. Mr Mealing was holding a mop of hair in his hand. Mr Brown had been wearing a wig!

"And I think that this is suspicious." Mr Mealing took hold of one end of the moustache and pulled – hard.

"Oooh, ahh!" cried Mr Brown as his moustache came off leaving sticky glue on his upper lip.

"And finally," crowed the headmaster as he tugged at the beard.

"Eeeeeee," screamed Mr Brown as his beard came off and he stood in front of Mr Mealing – not Mr Brown but Craig Webster, the naughtiest boy in the school.

"What is the meaning of this?" thundered the headmaster.

"It was a joke Sir," explained Craig.

"A joke! You call this a JOKE," and Mr Mealing looked around his study with all the papers on the floor and at the broken glass cabinet. "This is not what I call funny.

"It was a dare Sir. You can't refuse a dare."

"Well I will see you at lunch time about your JOKE and then I will get in touch with your parents about your behaviour. Someone will have to pay for the damage and it won't be me."

"Sorry Sir; I won't do it again," whined Craig but the headmaster just pointed to the door and Craig went out.

Chapter Five

Mr Mealing picked up his chair and sat down for a few minutes. He closed his eyes and tried not to notice his wrecked study. Then he opened the door and went outside to the next candidate.

"Good morning," he said. "Would you like to come into my office. Please excuse the mess."

The fair haired man followed Mr Mealing and, after looking at the chaos, picked up the waste paper bin, turned it upside down and sat upon it.

"Good morning," he said. "My name is Mr Noke and because I never grew tall I learnt three types of martial arts so that I would not be bullied. What is the job? The advertisement said that it might be dangerous."

"Before I tell you that," answered Mr Mealing, 'I need you to prove to me that you can do karate and that you are not just wasting my time."

"I can do this," stated Mr Noke and standing up he went to the empty desk and looked at it for a few seconds. Then he shouted, "Ah wah," lifted his hand up and brought the edge down upon the

centre of the table. There was a loud crack and the table split in two.

"Is that good enough?"

Mr Mealing looked at his broken table as if he could not believe his eyes.

"How did you do that?" he gasped. "You have definitely got the job! Let us have a coffee in the staff room and I'll tell you all about it."

He shook Mr Noke's hand and led him out of his wrecked study. As he went past the school secretary's office he opened the door.

"Mrs Wright. I am taking Mr Noke to the staff room and we are not to be disturbed. Do you think you could tidy up my office? It's in a bit of a mess. Thank you."

He then closed the door quickly before Mrs Wright had a chance to reply.

Once in the staff room Mr Mealing explained to Mr Noke that some children from the school had gone missing and that all the missing children were last seen walking down the lane at the back of the school.

"I would like you to dress up as a pupil and go down the lane on your own when school has finished. Because I do not know what is happening to the children you need to be able to look after yourself but I will give you a secret weapon."

Mr Mealing then reached into his pocket and drew out – a whistle. He gave it to Mr Noke.

"If there is any danger you are to blow upon this as loud as you can. My staff and I will be listening and we will come as fast as we can. (Which might not be very fast. Some of the teachers are getting a bit creaky.) The pay is £100 now and an extra £100 if you can find out what is happening to our children."

Mr Noke solemnly took the whistle and put it in his pocket.

"I accept the job. When do I start?"

"This afternoon," replied Mr Mealing. "I will get you a school uniform so that you will look like one of the children. Be ready to go down the lane at four o'clock. All the children will have left by then and maybe you can find out what is happening down there."

Chapter Six

At quarter to four that afternoon there was an air of tension in the school. The teachers all had their running shoes on ready to sprint towards the lane as soon as they heard a whistle.

Mr Noke wore a school fleece and was carrying a

book bag.   He had a hood on his head, pulled down to hide his face. He solemnly shook hands with the Headmaster; nodded to the rest of the staff and set off, alone, across the playground, over the school field and towards the gate that led to the lane.

Mrs Selwood (who taught drama) gave a loud sniff.

"That's a very brave man," she wavered. "I hope that we see him again."

Mr Noke was not feeling brave as he walked towards the lane. He was feeling rather silly carrying a book bag and hoped that none of his friends would see him. He opened the gate and looked down the lane. As far as he could see it was just an ordinary lane, a bit muddy in places, but if he walked carefully he would not get his feet wet.

On the other side of the hedge the dragon heard breathing. He sniffed. One person – good; small – good; smelt a bit tough but he was not particularly fussy. He unfurled his wings and flew over the hedge, landing in front of Mr Noke. He paused. He liked to see the look of surprise that came over his victim's faces before he ate them. Mr Noke did look surprised but he didn't look very scared. He didn't look very much like a child either. Whilst the dragon was thinking these thoughts he opened his mouth to breathe out fire. Quickly Mr Noke turned on his side, kicked out with his leg and hit the dragon straight in the throat. (This is not recommended for children to copy. They are likely to fall over and they will ALWAYS be told off).

The dragon gasped as the foot hit him and the fire and smoke went back into his own throat. Tears started to come out of his eyes and whilst he was choking Mr Noke pulled the whistle out of his pocket and blew!

The school doors opened and out ran the teachers. Some of them were carrying cricket bats, some rounder's bats and others skipping ropes. They came charging over the playing field, into the lane and stopped at the terrible sight of a real dragon blundering around (he could not see by now) breathing out smoke.

Then, "Come on staff," yelled Mr Mealing banishing his cricket bat, "Let's get him."

He rushed over to the dragon and hit him on his leg. The teachers followed and soon the dragon was being hit all over his body. Some of the teachers had the clever idea of tying his mouth up with the skipping ropes so that he could not open it to breathe out fire.

Mr Noke sat on top of the dragon's head giving him karate chops. His head was too thick for Mr Noke to break but the dragon was certainly getting a headache.

Mr Mealing called out to Mrs Wright, "Phone the army. Tell them there is a dragon loose."

Soon the sound of a hovering helicopter drowned out all the shouts and grunts coming from the lane. Mrs Selwood stopped hitting the dragon's hind leg with her handbag and watched as two ropes came out of the helicopter and five soldiers with guns strapped to their backs came down the

ropes. She decided that she was having a very exciting day – much better than teaching children!

"Stand back," the soldiers ordered and, as the teachers obeyed, they raised their rifles and fired. Of course they did not use real bullets. They could not kill the only dragon in the world. They used tranquilliser guns – the sort used to stop a charging rhinoceros. The dragon stopped fighting. A silly smile came over his face. All of a sudden he felt happy. Then he fell down unconscious.

When he came too he was in a large steel cage that had quickly been built around him. He had a very bad headache and an idea that the people looking at him were not pleased with him.

"Well dragon," said Mr Mealing. "What have you to say for yourself?"

The dragon decided that being honest was the only way he was going to get out of this situation.

"I was hungry Sir. There is nothing to eat in this field and I could not go to another field because I was scared of being seen. I am very sorry and I promise that I will not eat any more of your children – word of a dragon."

"It's alright saying 'Sorry' but you have done a very bad thing and you have to pay for it. What can you do to make amends?"

The dragon thought and then said in a very small voice, "I can't do much Sir. All I can do is breathe fire and fly."

The Headmaster thought for a long moment and then he smiled.

"We can use that ability. Our school is an old school with large Victorian pipes that go round the classrooms to heat them up. We have to heat up the water that go round the pipes and that costs us a lot of money. You could live in our boiler room and when it is cold you could breathe fire into the pipes and warm up the pipes for nothing. The money that we save could be used to build and equip a new I.C.T. suite and that would help all the children. We would feed you twice a day but you have to promise never to eat any more children. Is it a deal?"

Of course the dragon agreed and that day he went to live in his new home in the boiler house.

In a short time the children got used to him being there and they often spent their playtimes playing with him and scratching his forehead.

When the Summer Fayre arrived there was a new attraction. The dragon came out of the boiler house and had a special saddle placed on him – the type that elephants sometimes wear – with three seats for people on one side and three on the other. There was a sign saying:

Dragon Ride
£1 a go
Unique Opportunity

When the dragon was loaded up with six people he took off and flew around the school, over the village, past the big house, zoomed over the river, skimmed the fields and landed back safely ready for the next flight. He was the most popular attraction of the day and even had his photo taken for the local newspaper. At the end of the day he had made over one thousand pounds for the school. A record!

That night, after his dinner of pizza, pork chops and sausage rolls, he slept soundly in his boiler house – no longer a hungry dragon.

Oh, in case you are wondering about what happened to the mothers who had lost their children. They decided that they liked having their houses staying clean and tidy and their biscuit tins full so they were quite happy too.

THE END

Printed in Great Britain
by Amazon